Thomas the Tank Engine & Friends™

CREATED BY BRITT ALLCROFT

Based on The Railway Series by The Reverend W Awdry.
© 2008 Gullane (Thomas) LLC.

Thomas the Tank Engine & Friends and Thomas & Friends are trademarks of
Gullane (Thomas) Limited.

Thomas the Tank Engine & Friends & Design is Reg. U.S. Pat. & Tm. Off.

Published in the United States by Random House Children's Books,
a division of Random House, Inc., New York, and in Canada by
Random House of Canada Limited, Toronto.

Beginner Books, Random House, and the Random House colophon are registered
trademarks of Random House, Inc.

HIT entertainment

www.randomhouse.com/kids/thomas   www.thomasandfriends.com

Educators and librarians, for a variety of teaching tools, visit us at
www.randomhouse.com/teachers

Library of Congress Cataloging-in-Publication Data
Trains, cranes & troublesome trucks : a Thomas & Friends story /
illustrated by Tommy Stubbs. — 1st ed.
p. cm. — (Thomas & Friends)
"Based on The Railway Series by The Reverend W Awdry."
Summary: Thomas, James, and Gordon are determined to do their jobs for the day but the
Troublesome Trucks are just as determined to interfere and cause trouble for everyone.
ISBN 978-0-375-84977-0 (trade) — ISBN 978-0-375-94977-7 (lib. bdg.)
[1. Stories in rhyme. 2. Railroad trains—Fiction.] I. Stubbs, Tommy, ill.
II. Awdry, W. Railway series. III. Title: Trains, cranes and troublesome trucks.
PZ8.3.T682 2008   [E]—dc22   2007040838

Printed in the United States of America   9   First Edition

Trains, Cranes & Troublesome Trucks

A Thomas & Friends Story

**Based on *The Railway Series*
by The Reverend W Awdry**

Illustrated by Tommy Stubbs

BEGINNER BOOKS® A Division of Random House, Inc.

The sun comes up on trains and cranes
of many different sizes.
The Troublesome Trucks are also up . . .
up to no-good surprises.

Thomas, James, and Gordon
each must make a harbor run.
Small, medium, and big loads,
a job for everyone.
But the Troublesome Trucks
just want to have fun, fun, fun!

Today small Thomas has a goal.

Today he pulls dusty coal.

Thomas must go slow, slow, slow.

The Troublesome Trucks want to go, go, go!

Thomas peeps, "No, no, no!"

The Trucks push Thomas faster, faster.

The curve ahead could mean disaster.

Go, go, go, down the hill.

CRASH!

Oh, what a great big spill!

Thomas is off the track.

Harvey comes to lift him back.

Small engine, big trouble.

Small crane helps on the double.

Thomas can only grin and sigh

as James comes rushing by.

Medium-sized James pulls milk today.

He has no time to talk or play.

James must go slow, slow, slow.

The Troublesome Trucks want to go, go, go!

James toots, "No, no, no!"

The Trucks brake hard and then let go.

A jerky, jumpy ride. Oh, no!

They rock and roll, and with a . . .

SPLASH!

James has a great big crash!

Poor James is off the track.

Rocky comes to lift him back.

Medium engine, big trouble.

Medium crane helps on the double.

James can only grin and sigh
as Gordon comes rushing by.

Gordon is big. He pulls heavy freight.

He must be careful and not be late.

Gordon must go slow, slow, slow.

The Troublesome Trucks want to go, go, go!

Gordon chuffs, "No, no, no!"

Down to the Docks, they rush without care.

Before they know it, they are there.

At the end of the line, Gordon cannot stop.

BANG!

Into the bumper, the Trucks flip-flop.

Poor Gordon is off the track.

Cranky is there to lift him back.

Big engine, BIG trouble.

Big crane helps on the double.

Gordon can only sigh and grin

as James and Thomas both pull in.

Thomas, James, and Gordon
go back to the Yard.
Three dirty engines
have all worked hard.

They grumble, grumble, grumble
about those Troublesome Trucks.

Splish, splosh, splash.

Workers wash each one.

Small, medium, big—

the washing-up is fun.

Rub them down and make them shine . . .

then back to the Shed, looking fine.

The sun goes down on Thomas and friends.
A lesson was learned in the end.
When Trucks cause trouble,
just call on the cranes—
they are there on the double
to help all sizes of trains.

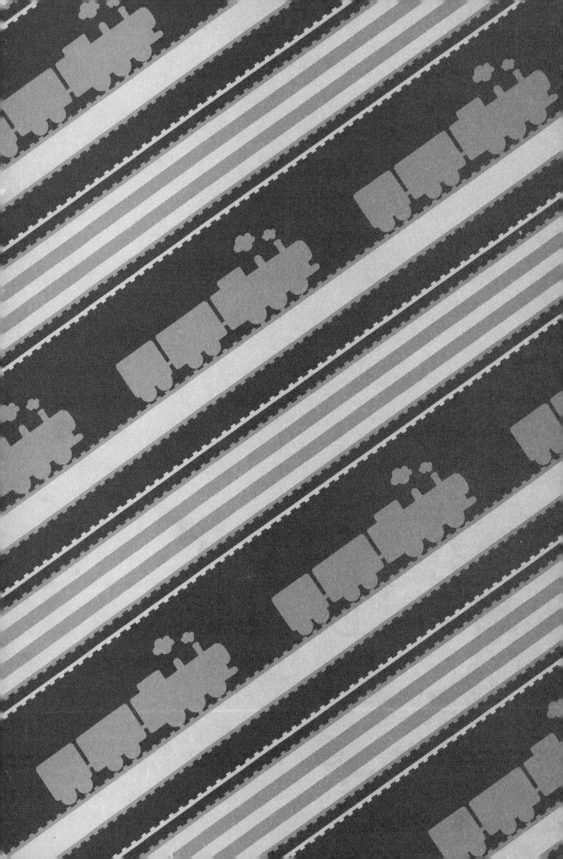